SCIENCE TIMES
WITH
NURSERY RHYMES

by
Stephanie K. Burton
and
Phyllis Campbell

Nursery Rhyme Illustrations
by
Eric Stambaugh

Panda Bear Publications
P.O. Box 391
Manitou Springs, CO 80829
ph: (719) 685-3319
fax: (719) 685-4427
www.pandabooks.com

Acknowledgements

From Stephanie:
Thank you, once again, to my wonderful husband Andrew and my patient children, Lindsey and Josh, for putting up with my long hours on the computer.

Thanks to my parents Norman and Lois Kay for encouraging me to set goals and see them through.

A special thank you to my educational assistants, Brenda, Maria and Carol for their unquestioning and unfailing support of my arts-based curriculum.

Thank you to my nephew Eric Stambaugh for the whimsical nursery rhyme illustrations.

Thanks, also, to my sister, Victoria Pappas, for helping Eric to complete his first professional art endeavor.

From Phyllis:
I wish to thank my husband Jim, and my son Sean for their love and encouragement always. Thanks for the confidence!

A special thank you to my parents Mary and Norman Vowell for their support and belief in me through the years.

Many thanks to Diane, Barb, and Clare for assisting and encouraging me daily in the classroom.

About the Authors

Stephanie Burton began her teaching career in 1980 after receiving an M.A.T. from The Colorado College. Her conviction that it is important to use the arts as a tool for learning the basics is reflected, not only in her classroom, but in her publications. Her first book MUSIC EXPLOSION received the 1994 Early Childhood News Award and her second book MUSIC MANIA is fast becoming a favorite among early childhood teachers. SCIENCE TIMES WITH NURSERY RHYMES combines the sense of rhythm and the fun of nursery rhymes with the exploration of scientific concepts introduced in each rhyme.

Phyllis Campbell has been working with young children since 1975. She graduated with a B.S. in Special Education and earned a Masters degree in Early Childhood Education from Auburn University. She has been teaching in Colorado Springs public school system since 1990. Mrs. Campbell has always believed that young children must touch and explore in order to learn. This belief, along with twenty years of practical experience and her knowledge of developmentally appropriate practices, provided her with the foundation for this book.

INTRODUCTION

Science and Young Children

Children are naturally curious about the world around them. They frequently ask questions such as, "How does that work," "Why does that happen?" and "What if..." Adults can help children to comprehend their world better by providing opportunities for them to explore and experiment in a safe, well-supervised environment.

Science with young children should encourage exploration with materials that will lead them to make their own discoveries. For concepts to have meaning for young children they must be allowed to manipulate and investigate these objects and materials. By permitting them the freedom to observe, touch and test, children are best able to form their own conclusions. This type of active learning has more meaning and permanence than a passive learning experience where children are just observers or simply learning by rote memorization.

In a developmentally appropriate science environment you will see children excited about learning at the level that best fits each child's own stage of development. It is for this reason that it is important that the science activities be open-ended with possibilities for expansion as the children look for opportunities for further investigation.

If you are teaching young children in a classroom setting, it is important that you *always* have a science area set up with materials for children to explore. Sometimes you may want to have materials that are simply for observation such as rocks, leaves, or other items from nature. Other times you will want to provide materials that invite exploration *and* experimentation, such as magnets with magnetic and non-magnetic items, cornstarch and water, colored water and droppers, or baking soda and vinegar. It is also appropriate to occasionally conduct science experiments with the children in a more formal group setting. If it is possible for the children to safely follow-up a formal science experiment by manipulating the materials or objects themselves, it is important to give them that opportunity.

How to Use This Book

Each science activity contains these sections:

Nursery Rhyme- In **SCIENCE TIMES WITH NURSERY RHYMES,** scientific investigation is preceded by the presentation of a popular nursery rhyme. Subsequently, the scientific concepts found in each nursery rhyme are explored in a variety of science investigation activities. Teachers may find that rather than "jumping in" to a science activity, the reading and discussion of the nursery rhyme will help to capture the young child's attention and can naturally lead to scientific investigation. For example, after reading the poem "Jack and Jill" you might ask the children why did Jack fall down instead of falling up? This, of course, would lead to discussion and experimentation with the effects of gravity.

What The Children Will Learn- This will tell you the goal or objective of each activity.

You Will Need- Gather these materials together before embarking on an activity. Most of the ingredients are commonly found in your home or school.

Try This- This is the step-by-step description of the science experience. It is often a good idea to try the activity on your own so that you know how it works before sharing it with the students.

Why Does It Work?- This is an explanation in layman's terms of why the experiment works.

TABLE OF CONTENTS

HEY DIDDLE DIDDLE

Hey diddle diddle,

The cat and the fiddle,

The cow jumped over the moon;

The little dog laughed

to see such sport;

And the dish ran away

with the spoon.

FIDDLIN' AROUND

<u>WHAT THE CHILDREN WILL LEARN:</u>
Sounds are made from vibrations.

<u>YOU WILL NEED:</u>
      Empty tissue boxes, shoe boxes, aluminum
          or tin pie pans
      Rubber bands of varying thicknesses
      Markers, stickers, construction paper, glue
      Paint sticks (paint stores will donate these)

<u>TRY THIS!</u>
1. Decorate the boxes or pie tins with stickers, construction paper, and markers.
2. Stretch rubber bands lengthwise across the opening.
3. Glue or tape the paint stick to the back of the box or tin so that it extends out like the neck of a fiddle or guitar. (This step is optional.)
4. Experiment with the sound by stretching the rubber bands as you pluck them and noticing the various pitches you hear.

<u>WHY DOES IT WORK?</u>
The vibrations from the rubber bands resonate in the hollow space of the box or tin. Stretching the rubber bands raises the pitch of the sound.

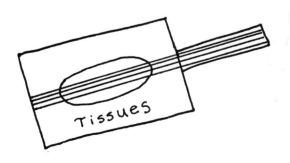

SPOON CHIMES

<u>WHAT THE CHILDREN WILL LEARN:</u>
Sound vibrations travel through string.

<u>YOU WILL NEED:</u>
   Spoon
   Piece of string (about a yard long)

<u>TRY THIS!</u>
1. Tie a spoon in the middle of the string.
2. Wind the two ends of the string around your forefingers.
3. Place the tips of the forefingers in your ears.
5. Dangle the spoon so that it hits against a hard object. You'll hear a sound like a chime.
6. VARIATION: Try this experiment using different objects.

<u>WHY DOES IT WORK?</u>
The sound vibrations caused by the spoon striking a hard object travel up the string. That sound is conducted up through the string, through your fingers and directly to the eardrums.

SOUND SHAKERS

WHAT THE CHILDREN WILL LEARN:
Sound will vary according to the material and quantity used.

YOU WILL NEED:
    2 paper plates or aluminum pie tins
    Beans, paper clips, marbles, or other
        materials to make sounds
    Glue, tape or staples
    Collage materials
    Markers

TRY THIS!
1. Place a handful of the sound making materials (beans, paper clips, etc.) in one of the plates or tins.
2. Place the second plate or tin upside down onto the first plate. Glue, staple or tape the rims together.
3. Decorate the shaker with markers, stickers, or collage material.
4. Guess what materials were used in the different shakers by listening to the sound they make.

9

LOOK AT THE SOUND

WHAT THE CHILDREN WILL LEARN:
Sound waves are vibrations that travel through the air.

YOU WILL NEED:
   Large cake or cookie tin
   Piece of plastic tarp or shower curtain
   Heavy duty rubber band
   Cookie baking tray
   Wooden Spoon
   Brown Sugar

TRY THIS!
1. Stretch the plastic tightly over the top opening of the cake or cookie tin.
2. Place the rubber band over the plastic to hold it securely in place on the tin.
3. Sprinkle about a teaspoon of brown sugar on top of the tin "drum" you have created.
4. Hold the cookie baking tray close to, but not touching, the drum.
5. Tap the cookie baking tray sharply with the wooden spoon.
6. Watch the brown sugar dancing on the drum head.

WHY DOES IT WORK?
When you strike the metal tray, the vibrations (*sound waves*) travel through the surrounding air. When the sound waves hit the drum head it causes the sugar to vibrate and "dance." When the sound waves hit your ear, you hear the sound of the spoon hitting the tray.

MUSICAL WATER GLASSES

WHAT THE CHILDREN WILL LEARN:
Pitch is affected by airspace.

YOU WILL NEED:
   4-8 Water glasses (same size and type)
   Water
   Metal spoon

TRY THIS!
1. Put water glasses in a row.
2. Fill the glasses with decreasing amounts of water.
3. Gently tap the water glasses with a metal spoon.
4. Listen to the different pitches caused by the varying amounts of water.
5. If you have 8 glasses, you can adjust the amount of water in the glasses to produce a scale. Play some songs on them.

WHY DOES IT WORK?
The lesser the amount of airspace in each glass the higher the pitch.

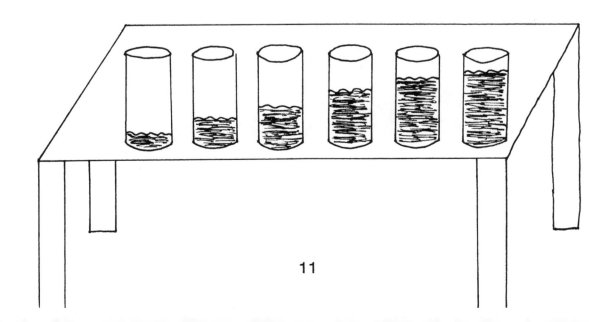

THEME INTEGRATION

Sound/Five Senses
Animals
Water

RELATED SONGS AND RHYMES

Pussy Cat, Pussy Cat
Old Mother Hubbard
Did You Feed My Cow
Old MacDonald

RELATED LITERATURE

I Went Walking- Sue Williams
Papa, Please Get the Moon For Me - Eric Carle
The Three Little Kittens - Lorinda Cauley

HICKORY, DICKORY, DOCK

Hickory, dickory, dock,

The mouse ran up the clock.

The clock struck one,

The mouse ran down,

Hickory, dickory, dock.

THE PENDULUM

<u>WHAT THE CHILDREN WILL LEARN:</u>
The length of a piece of string determines the speed at which a pendulum will swing.

<u>YOU WILL NEED:</u>
Kite string - 15-20 inches
Washer
Tape
Stop watch
Table

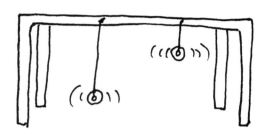

<u>TRY THIS!</u>
1. Tape one end of the string to the edge of the table.
2. Tie the washer to the other end of the string.
3. The string should hang straight down.
4. Pull the washer up toward the table. Release the string and, using the stop watch, count the number of swings for a given amount of time.
5. Shorten the string by 3/4 and try the experiment again.
6. The number of swings the pendulum makes should double.

<u>WHY DOES IT WORK?</u>
The speed of the swing of a pendulum depends on the length of the string. The time decreases by half when the string is 3/4 its original length. Galileo was the first person to discover this principal.

PULL THE NAIL

WHAT THE CHILDREN WILL LEARN:
The claw of a hammer is a simple machine and demonstrates a first class lever.

YOU WILL NEED:
    Block of wood or tree stump
    Claw hammers
    Roofing nails
    Safety goggles

TRY THIS!
1. Have children wear goggles before using a hammer and nails.
2. Allow children to pound nails into wood.
3. Use the claw to remove the nails from the wood.

WHY DOES IT WORK?
A lever is a simple machine that allows you to perform work that otherwise could not be accomplished. The claw is placed under the nail (*the load*). It is braced against the wood (*the fulcrum*) and when the child pushes down on the handle (*the effort*) the nail is lifted out of the wood.

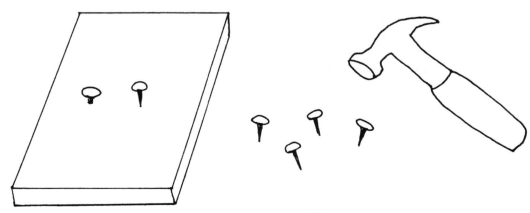

CATCH THE BEAN BAG

WHAT THE CHILDREN WILL LEARN:
The catapult is a simple machine called a *lever*.

YOU WILL NEED:
- 1x4 inch board -30" long
- 2x2 inch block of wood
- Nails
- Bean bag
- Permanent marking pen

TRY THIS!
1. Sand both pieces of wood.
2. Nail the board to the block 6-8 inches from the end of the board.
3. Turn the board so that it stands on the small block of wood. It should look like a lop-sided see-saw.
4. Draw an X on the long end of the see-saw. This will show the child where to place the bean bag.
5. Place the bean bag on the X. Stand at the short end of the catapult. Quickly step onto the short end of the board. The bean bag should shoot straight up into the air.
6. Catch the bean bag!

WHY DOES IT WORK?
This is an example of a first class lever. The bean bag is the *load*, the small block of wood is the *fulcrum*, and the pressure on the short end of the board is the *effort*. The fulcrum allows the lever to pivot. Pushing down quickly on the short end of the board forces the long end up and the bean bag shoots up into the air.

MOVE THE BOX

WHAT THE CHILDREN WILL LEARN:
Heavy objects can be moved easily when friction is reduced.

YOU WILL NEED:
        Large cardboard box
        7 - 10 dowels (1/4 inch)
        Rope
        Blocks

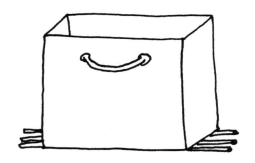

TRY THIS!
1. Cut two holes in front of the box and attach the rope.
2. Have children pull the box to show how easily the box can be moved when empty.
3. Load the box with blocks and have the children try and pull it across the room. Friction should keep the box from moving more than a few inches.
4. Lay the dowels on the floor about 2 inches apart.
5. Place the box on top of the dowels and have the children try to pull the box. It should move easily now.

WHY DOES IT WORK?
The bottom of the box is in total contact with the floor. As it is pulled, resistance (*friction*) is produced. A rolling object creates little friction because of limited contact with the floor. The box moves easily on the rolling dowels because there is little resistance against the floor and the box.

TUG OF BROOMS!

WHAT WILL CHILDREN LEARN?
It is easier to move objects with the help of a pulley. A pulley is a simple machine.

YOU WILL NEED:
    2 brooms
    Rope - 4-5 feet long
    3 children

TRY THIS!
1. 2 children should hold the brooms lengthwise about 20 inches apart.
2. Tie the rope near the end of one broom.
3. Wrap the rope around the brooms once, keeping the brooms apart.
4. Have the third child pull the free end of the rope while the other two children try to keep the brooms apart.
5. The child should be able to pull the brooms together.
6. Try this again. This time, wrap the rope around the brooms 3 times. Try to keep the brooms apart.
7. The brooms should pull together very easily.

WHY DOES IT WORK?
This is an example of a simple machine known as a *pulley*. Pulleys work to change the direction and point of application of a pulling force in order to move an object. The force needed to pull the brooms together is multiplied by the number of ropes attached to the brooms. Wrapping the rope around the brooms allows the brooms to be pulled together easily even when great resistance is applied.

THEME INTEGRATION

Machines
Time
Animals
Containers
Spatial Concepts - in/out, up/down, high/low
Transportation

RELATED SONGS AND RHYMES

My Grandfather's Clock
Three Blind Mice
Old Mother Hubbard
Over In The Meadow
One, Two, Buckle My Shoe
Machines and Things That Go - Jon Fromer

RELATED LITERATURE

The Grouchy Ladybug - Eric Carle
May I Bring A Friend - Beatrice DeRegniers
Dig, Drill, Dump, Fill - Tana Hoban
Machines At Work - Bryon Barton
The Bridge - Emily Cheney Neville

HUMPTY-DUMPTY

Humpty-Dumpty sat on a wall,

Humpty-Dumpty had a great fall;

All the king's horses

And all the king's men,

Couldn't put Humpty together

again.

"EGG-CITING" TASTE FESTIVAL

WHAT THE CHILDREN WILL LEARN:
Eggs can be prepared many different ways and each tastes different. Here are a few suggestions: egg salad (see recipe that follows), hard-boiled eggs, fried eggs, scrambled eggs

YOU WILL NEED:
EGG SALAD (recipe follows)

EGG SALAD (for 15 children)
8 hard-boiled eggs
mayonnaise
pinch of salt

Prepare the hard-boiled eggs ahead of time. The children can peel the eggs. Ask the children to chop the egg into small pieces using a butter knife. Add enough mayonnaise to make a smooth consistency. (You can hard boil the eggs a day or two ahead of time and add the mayo right before serving.) Mix thoroughly. Add a pinch of salt. Refrigerate if not serving immediately.

TRY THIS!
After the children have tasted eggs prepared several different ways, graph their preferences.

HOW DO YOU PREFER YOUR EGGS?

egg salad	hard-boiled	fried	scrambled
Sarah	Mary	Sean	Josh
Andrew	Lindsey		Paulie
	Jim		Nancy

EGG DROP

<u>WHAT THE CHILDREN WILL LEARN:</u>
Proper packaging can protect a fragile egg when dropped from various heights.

<u>YOU WILL NEED:</u>
   Fresh eggs
   Containers and boxes of various shapes and sizes
   Insulators i.e. foam packing, tissue, bubble wrap,
         confetti, cotton, paper towels, etc.
   Duct tape or packing tape

<u>TRY THIS!</u>
1. Drop an egg from the top of a ladder and watch how easily the egg breaks. (Do this outside or drop it on a some newspaper to make clean-up easier!)
2. Show the children the construction materials and ask them to develop a container to protect the egg from breaking when it is dropped.
3. Have children work in small groups to construct their inventions. Additional adults may be needed.
4. An egg should be placed in each box when the inventions are complete. Repeat step 1. Record which boxes prevented the egg from breaking and which boxes did not.
5. Discuss with the children why they think one design worked better than another. What suggestions do they have to improve their designs?
6. VARIATION: Have the children design a soft landing surface for an unprotected egg. Try dropping the egg onto the surface from different heights until it breaks.

<u>WHY DOES IT WORK?</u>
The box and insulating material work as a shock absorber. They reduce the impact of the fall by displacing the energy across the surface of the box and by absorbing the energy up through the box.

EGG IN A BOTTLE

WHAT THE CHILDREN WILL LEARN:
Vacuum pressure can force a hard-boiled egg through a narrow opening.

YOU WILL NEED:
   Glass jar (with opening narrow enough for
      egg to rest on)
   Hard-boiled egg with shell removed
   Paper
   Matches

TRY THIS!
1. Place a hard-boiled egg on the opening of the jar to demonstrate that the egg won't fall through.
2. Remove the egg.
3. Light the paper as you place it inside the jar.
4. Place the egg in the opening of the jar so that it creates a seal.
6. As the oxygen is used up by the burning paper, a vacuum will be created which will force the egg to be pulled inside the bottle.

WHY DOES IT WORK?
The fire uses up the available oxygen in the bottle. This creates a vacuum inside the bottle. Air outside the bottle pushes down against the egg, forcing the egg into the bottle.

RUBBER EGG

WHAT THE CHILDREN WILL LEARN:
The vinegar causes a chemical reaction with the eggshell resulting in a rubbery egg.

YOU WILL NEED:
　　1 raw egg in its shell
　　Jar or small bowl
　　White vinegar

TRY THIS!
1. Observe the egg in the shell and record children's comments.
2. Place the egg carefully inside the jar so as not to crack the shell.
3. Cover the egg with vinegar.
4. Record the children's observations periodically over the next 72 hours.
5. Remove the egg after 72 hours.
6. Record the children's observations of the changes that have taken place.

WHY DOES IT WORK?
A chemical reaction occurs between the eggshell which is made of limestone (calcium carbonate) and the vinegar. One of the changes produces carbon dioxide, hence the bubbles on the egg. The thickness of the egg shell is reduced. The egg shell does not disappear, but becomes rubbery.

DYE IT NATURALLY

WHAT THE CHILDREN WILL LEARN:
How to color hard-boiled eggs using natural
dyes.

YOU WILL NEED:

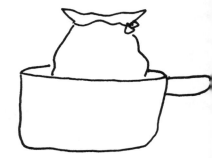

Raw Eggs	Beet skins
String	Orange peels
Cheesecloth	Potato peels
Water	Onion skins
Pot	Radish skins

TRY THIS!
1. Place 3 to 4 eggs and your choice of
   peelings from the list above in a bag made of
   cheesecloth tied with string. You can use one
   type of peel or use a combination.
2. Cook the eggs and peels in the cheesecloth
   bag until hard-boiled.
3. Carefully remove the bags from the water
   and let cool.
4. After it has cooled, let the children remove
   the eggs from the cheesecloth bags. Observe
   the colors on the shells.

WHY DOES IT WORK?
Eggshells are porous. The color in the peels leaks
out into the water where it is absorbed by the
eggshell.

THEME INTEGRATION

Eggs
Outer Space/Gravity
Air/Wind
Spring Time
Colors

RELATED SONGS AND RHYMES

Jack and Jill
Baby Bird

RELATED LITERATURE

Good Morning, Chick - Mirra Ginsburg
Seven Eggs - Meredith Cooper
Little Monsters: Eggs for Tea -Jan Pienkowski
Max's Chocolate Chicken - Rosemary Wells

I'M A LITTLE TEAPOT

I'm a little teapot short and stout,

Here is my handle,

Here is my spout.

When I get all steamed up,

Hear me shout,

"Tip me over and pour me out!"

DON'T GET STEAMED!

WHAT THE CHILDREN WILL LEARN:
Heated water changes into an invisible gas called *steam*. As the steam cools, it changes from a gas back into liquid water.

YOU WILL NEED:
Plastic zipper bag - 1 per child
Water
Tape
Food coloring (optional)

TRY THIS!
1. Fill half of the zipper bag with warm water.
2. Add 1-2 drops of food coloring.
3. Close the bag and tape it to a sunny window.
4. Check the bag after 15 minutes. Water droplets should be visible in the top half of the bag.

WHY DOES IT WORK?
The sun and the heat from the water changes some of the water into an invisible gas or vapor called steam. The steam is warm and rises to the top of the bag. As it cools, the air can hold less and less water vapor. The gas changes back into tiny drops of water. This is the *water cycle*.

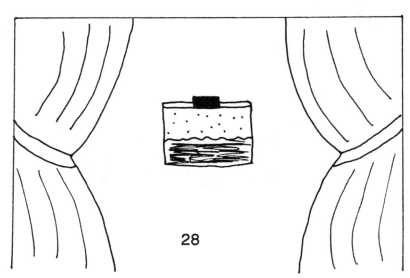

ESCAPING GAS

←balloon filled with baking soda

Vinegar

WHAT THE CHILDREN WILL LEARN:
Some solids and liquids can be mixed together to form a gas.

YOU WILL NEED:
   Vinegar
   Baking soda
   1 or 2 liter plastic bottle
   Balloon
   Funnel

TRY THIS!
1. Attach the neck of the balloon onto the end of a funnel.
2. Pour a tablespoon of baking soda into the balloon.
3. Using the funnel, pour about an inch of vinegar into the bottle. Don't worry about exact measurements. That is half the fun of this experiment!
4. Attach the neck of the balloon onto the bottle opening.
5. Raise the balloon, allowing the baking soda to fall into the bottle.
6. Was enough gas created from the chemical reaction of the two ingredients to inflate the balloon?

WHY DOES IT WORK?
The vinegar and baking soda create a chemical reaction which produces a gas called *carbon dioxide*. The gas is released when the bubbles pop and the air is trapped inside the balloon. The air pushes against the sides of the balloon and the balloon inflates.

THE SHAPE OF WATER

WHAT THE CHILDREN WILL LEARN:
Water changes from a liquid to a solid when
frozen. Water changes its shape in liquid form.

YOU WILL NEED:
     Various sizes and shapes of containers
     Water
     Food coloring (optional)
     Freezer

TRY THIS!
1. Mix the water with food coloring.
2. Pour the water into various containers. Notice
     how the water in the liquid state takes the
     shape of each container.
3. Place containers in freezer for several hours.
4. Remove the frozen water from the containers.
5. The water is now solid. Notice how the solid
     water (*ice*) retains its shape.

WHY DOES IT WORK?
A liquid is a substance that does not have its own
shape. It will take the form of whatever shape in
which it is placed. A solid is a substance that has
definite form and shape. As water is cooled, the
molecules slow down and expand. The water
changes from a liquid into a solid shape.

STOP THE MELTDOWN!

WHAT THE CHILDREN WILL LEARN:
Water changes from a solid into a liquid as it warms. Certain materials can be used to slow the warming process.

YOU WILL NEED:
>   Ice from the previous experiment
>   Various types of materials for insulation -
>   paper, plastic wrap, aluminum foil,
>   bubble wrap, cloth, socks, etc.
>   Containers for the solid water

TRY THIS!
1. Take the ice and wrap each piece in a different material.
2. Place the wrapped ice in a container to catch the water as it changes back into a liquid state.
3. Set the containers in different places around the room.
4. Observe the ice throughout the day.
5. Keep a record about the results of the ice meltdown. Which material provided the best insulation? How long did it take to melt the largest block of ice? Which material was least effective? Did certain places in the room effect the meltdown process?

WHY DOES IT WORK?
As the air around the ice warms, water changes into a vapor and back into a liquid. The longer water stays cold, the slower the change back to a liquid will be. Certain materials keep the cold in and around the ice, thus slowing the melting process.

PUD PLAY

WHAT THE CHILDREN WILL LEARN:
Water can be changed back and forth from a solid to a liquid state without freezing and melting.

YOU WILL NEED:
  Corn starch
  Water
  Food coloring (optional)
  Large pan or tray with sides

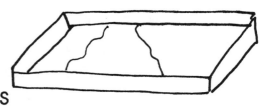

TRY THIS!
1. Pour corn starch onto a tray or pan.
2. Add colored water, small amounts at a time and mix with hands.
3. Continue adding and mixing water to get a smooth consistency. It should look like thick milk.
4. Allow the mixture to sit out overnight. The corn starch absorbs all the water and the pud is now a solid.
5. Add water to the mixture and it becomes a liquid again.
6. Do not worry about the mess! When the corn starch dries, it can easily be brushed off clothes and hands.

WHY DOES IT WORK?
Corn starch is a thickening agent. When the right amount of water is added, some of the liquid is absorbed and the mixture changes into a semi-solid. It becomes thick, but not thick enough to retain its shape. Left alone, the starch will absorb all the water and it will go back to its solid state once again.

THEME INTEGRATIONS

Air/Wind
Containers
Water
Weather
Food/Cooking
Matter- Solids, Liquids, Gases

RELATED SONGS AND RHYMES

Polly Put the Kettle On
Pease Porridge
Pat-A-Cake
Little Jack Horner
Sing A Song of Sixpence

RELATED LITERATURE

The Giant Jam Sandwich - John Vernon Lord
Stone Soup - Tony Ross
Strega Nona - Tomie DePaola

<u>JACK AND JILL</u>

Jack and Jill went up the hill,

To fetch a pail of water;

Jack fell down,

And broke his crown,

And Jill came tumbling after.

DON'T SPILL THE WATER!

WHAT THE CHILDREN WILL LEARN:
Air is strong. When enough pressure is applied, objects will stay inside a bucket, even upside-down.

YOU WILL NEED:
    Bucket with handle
    Variety of small objects
    Water

TRY THIS!
1. Place small objects (paper clips, blocks,etc.) inside of bucket.
2. Slowly swing bucket overhead, stopping when the bucket is upside-down. Items should fall to the ground. (This would be a good time to discuss gravity.)
3. Swing the bucket quickly overhead, making a complete circle. The objects should stay in the bucket.
4. Try using different objects in the bucket.
5. Fill bucket 1/3 with water. The water should stay in the rapidly spinning bucket.

WHY DOES IT WORK?
This is known as *centrifugal force*. Air pushes against the objects inside the bucket. As the bucket spins, greater pressure is exerted onto the objects. The objects are held in place by air pressure.

WATER FOUNTAIN

WHAT THE CHILDREN WILL LEARN
Water has weight. The pressure of the water increases as water becomes deeper.

YOU WILL NEED:
   2 liter plastic bottle
   Masking tape
   Water

TRY THIS!
   (You may want to try this experiment outside!)
1. Punch 3-4 holes in the side of the plastic bottle.
2. Cover the holes with a strip of masking tape.
3. Fill the bottle with water.
4. Remove the tape and watch the water spurt out of the holes.
5. The hole closest to the bottom of the bottle should have the strongest jet of water while the top hole should have a short, weak stream of water.

WHY DOES IT WORK?
Water has weight. This is known as water pressure. As the depth of water increases, more weight or pressure is exerted onto the water. The deeper the water, the greater the pressure.

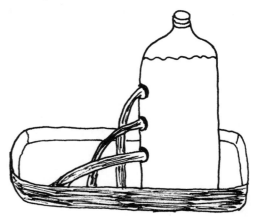

FLOAT OR SINK

WHAT THE CHILDREN WILL LEARN:
Objects which weigh less than water (are less dense) will float on the surface of the water. Objects which weigh more than water (are more dense) will sink.

YOU WILL NEED:
>   Container of water - dishpan or bucket
>   Variety of objects - try to find similar objects
>   of different sizes: blocks, toy cars, rocks
>   Fruits and vegetables

TRY THIS!
1. Fill the container 2/3 with water.
2. Pick out an object and ask children to predict whether the object will float (stay on top of the water) or sink (go to the bottom of the water).
3. Place an object in the water and watch.
4. What effect does size have on an object's ability to sink or float? Try two sizes of wood, plastic, metal. Are the results the same or different?
5. Place fruits and vegetables in the water. You may be surprised to find out which ones will sink and which will float!

WHY DOES IT WORK?
All objects have weight or mass. An object weighing less than the weight of water is said to be less dense than water and will float on top. If an object weighs more than water, it is more dense and will sink to the bottom.

IS THE GLASS REALLY FULL?

WHAT THE CHILDREN WILL LEARN:
Water has something like a tight skin stretched across it. This tension keeps water from overflowing a container.

YOU WILL NEED:
Container of water
Straight pins
Coins
Toothpicks

Any or all of these objects

TRY THIS!
1. Fill the container to the brim with water.
2. Add straight pins, one at a time, to the water. The water should bulge at the top but not overflow.
3. How many pins can the container hold before breaking the surface tension?
4. Try this experiment again using coins or toothpicks. What happened? Did the water hold more coins or more pins?

WHY DOES IT WORK?
The surface of water acts as if it has a tight skin stretched across it. This tightness that holds the surface of liquids together is called *surface tension.*

BUBBLE FUN

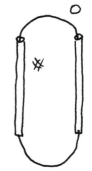

WHAT THE CHILDREN WILL LEARN:
Bubbles are created when surface tension is reduced and the water is stretched without breaking.

YOU WILL NEED:
- Dishwashing liquid (Dawn or Joy works best)
- Container of water
- Variety of objects with holes (bubble blowers, six pack holders)
- Drinking straws
- String

- Cheesecloth
- Rubber bands

TRY THIS!
(THIS WORKS BEST ON DAYS WITH HIGH HUMIDITY!)

1. Add LOTS of dishwashing detergent to container of water. Don't skimp with the detergent.
2. Experiment with various objects, dipping them into the bubble solution and blowing gently.
3. Make a large bubble blower. Take 16 inches of string and thread 2 straws onto the string. Tie ends together. Hold a straw in each hand, creating a large hoop. Dip the hoop into the bubble solution and gently blow or wave the hoop through the air.
4. Cut a 2 inch square from cheesecloth. Attach 2-3 layers of cheesecloth to the end of a straw. Secure with a rubber band. Dip cheesecloth end of straw into bubble solution and blow gently. The bubbles come through the holes in the cloth forming a long, strong chain of bubbles.

WHY DOES IT WORK?
Dishwashing liquid lessens the surface tension of the water. The surface can then be stretched farther before breaking. This stretched surface tension is known as bubbles.

THEME INTEGRATIONS

Air/Wind
Containers
Outer Space/Gravity
Water

RELATED SONGS AND RHYMES

Rain, Rain Go Away
It's Raining, It's Pouring
The Wind
Eensy, Weensy Spider
Rub A Dub Dub
Row, Row, Row Your Boat

RELATED LITERATURE

Rain - Peter Spiers
Amos and Boris - William Steig
Berenstain Bears Go To The Moon -
Stan Berenstain
Windsongs and Rainbows - Burton Albert

JACK BE NIMBLE

Jack be nimble,

Jack be quick,

Jack jump over the candlestick.

CANDLE-MAKING
(REQUIRES CLOSE ADULT SUPERVISION!)

WHAT THE CHILDREN WILL LEARN:
Candles are made out of several layers of warm liquid wax which is then cooled to become a solid.

YOU WILL NEED:
  Paraffin wax (available at hardware, grocery or craft stores)
  Peeled crayons for color
  Aluminum can
  Saucepan 1/2 full of water
  Cotton string or candle wicking
  Pencil or ruler to hold wick

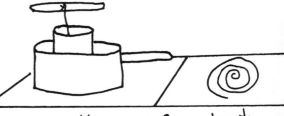

Remove the wax from heat as soon as it is melted

TRY THIS!
1. Cut the paraffin into chunks.
2. Fill the can 2/3 full of water.
3. Fill the saucepan 1/2 full of water.
4. Put the can into the saucepan. Place the paraffin into the can and add some pieces of peeled crayon for color.
5. Heat until the wax melts.
  (WARNING: NEVER MELT WAX DIRECTLY OVER HEAT!)
6. Cut a piece of string twice the length of the can. Attach the string to the middle of the pencil by either a knot or tape.
7. Remove the wax from the heat as soon as it is melted.
8. Dip the string into the wax. Lift it out and let it cool slightly before dipping it again.
  DO NOT TOUCH THE HOT WAX!!
  Repeat this process of dipping and cooling as often as you like until the candle is the size you want.
  (*Do not leave the candle in the warm wax too long or you'll melt the candle you've already built.*)
9. When finished, place the warm candle on a flat surface to flatten the bottom so that it will stand.

THE OXYGEN CONNECTION
(EXPERIMENT TO BE PERFORMED ONLY BY AN ADULT)

WHAT THE CHILDREN WILL LEARN:
Fire needs oxygen to survive. Without oxygen the fire goes out.

YOU WILL NEED:

    Candle
    Matches
    Wide-mouth jar or glass into which
        candle fits
    Flat dish or jar lid

TRY THIS!
1. Fix the candle onto the plate or the jar lid with some melted wax.
2. Light the candle.
3. Let the candle burn for about a minute then cover it with the glass or jar.
4. Count with the children to determine how long the candle stays burning before it goes out.
5. Have the children brainstorm ideas on why the candle goes out,
6. *Variation:* Try this with different size jars and the same size candle or different size candles and the same size jar. What factors change the amount of time the candle burns?

WHY DOES IT WORK?
Fire needs oxygen to continue to burn. The glass or jar initially contains oxygen from the air. As the candle burns, the fire uses up the available oxygen in the glass. When the oxygen is used up, the candle goes out.

BENDING AIR
(REQUIRES CLOSE ADULT SUPERVISION)

WHAT THE CHILDREN WILL LEARN:
Air currents bend around objects.

YOU WILL NEED:
>   Candle in a holder
>   Matches
>   Glass jar larger than the candle
>   Drinking straw

TRY THIS!
1. Place the glass jar in front of the candle in the candle holder.
2. The teacher or another adult lights the candle.
3. A child can blow through the drinking straw directly aimed at the front of the glass jar which has been placed in front of the candle.
4. The air will bend around the glass and extinguish the candle flame.

WHY DOES IT WORK?
Air currents bend around obstacles. Even though the air stream is directed toward the front of the glass jar, it goes around the glass and reaches the candle.

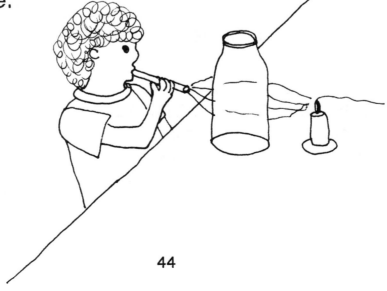

CREATE A VACUUM
(REQUIRES CLOSE ADULT SUPERVISION)

WHAT CHILDREN WILL LEARN:
When the air trapped inside a jar is used up by a burning flame, it creates a vacuum.

YOU WILL NEED:
   Candle
   Large glass jar
   Shallow dish
   Water (colored water works well)
   Matches

TRY THIS!
1. Secure the candle to the dish with melted wax.
2. Fill the shallow dish 3/4 full of water. Make sure that the candle is quite a bit higher than the water.
3. Light the candle.
4. Let the candle burn for a minute. Then place the glass jar upside-down over the burning candle. Do this at a slight angle so that some air is expelled as you lower the glass.
5. Notice the water level.
6. Watch what happens to the water level as the candle burns. When the flame goes out, the water level inside the jar has risen.

WHY DOES IT WORK?
When the oxygen inside the jar is used up by the burning candle, the flame goes out. Since there is now less air inside the jar than outside, a vacuum is created. Air pushes down against the water forcing the water up into the jar.

MAGIC PICTURES

WHAT THE CHILDREN WILL LEARN:
Wax resists water.

YOU WILL NEED:
   Candles
   White paper
   Watercolors or tempera thinned with water

TRY THIS!
1. Encourage the children to draw on the white paper with the candles. They will not be able to see what they have drawn!
2. Paint over the paper with watery watercolors or with the watered down tempera.
3. Watch the pictures emerge as if by magic!

WHY DOES IT WORK?
Candles are made of wax which is non-porous. When the water-based paint is spread over the areas that were drawn on with wax, the wax repels or resists the paint and shows through.

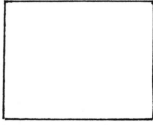

Drawing with candle wax

Candle wax drawing painted with watery tempera or watercolors

THEME INTEGRATION

Air/Wind
Light

RELATED SONGS AND RHYMES

The North Wind Doth Blow
One Light, One Sun
This Little Light Of Mine
Jumping Joan

RELATED LITERATURE

One Light, One Sun - Raffi
Quick as a Cricket - Dan and Audrey Wood
First Pink Light - Eloise Greenfield

LITTLE MISS MUFFET

Little Miss Muffet sat on a tuffet,
Eating her curds and whey.
Along came a spider,
Who sat down beside her,
And frightened Miss Muffet away.

CURDS AND WHEY

WHAT THE CHILDREN WILL LEARN:
Curds and whey are similar to store-bought cottage cheese (the process is more involved). Milk can be separated into solids and liquids.

YOU WILL NEED:
    Small baby food jars
    Fresh milk
    Vinegar (2 Tbs. for each jar)
    Tablespoon

TRY THIS!
1. Fill the jar with milk.
2. Add 2 Tbs. vinegar to the milk and stir.
3. Let milk mixture stand for 2-3 minutes.
4. Observe how the milk has separated into liquids and solids.

WHY DOES IT WORK?
Milk is an example of a *colloid,* a mixture of liquids and very tiny solid particles spread throughout. Vinegar causes the particles to group together forming solid clumps referred to as *curds. Whey* is what the liquid is called.

OBSERVING SPIDERS

<u>WHAT CHILDREN WILL LEARN:</u>
How spiders live and move in captivity.

<u>YOU WILL NEED:</u>
    A plastic bug jar-make your own or buy one
        (A peanut butter jar works well. Put air holes in
        the top. Place sticks and a damp sponge inside
        the jar.)
    A spider

<u>TRY THIS!</u>
1. Catch a spider and place it in the bug jar.
2. Place the jar where children can observe it.
3. Occasionally you will need to provide the spiders with insects to eat.
4. Keep paper, pencil and markers available near the spider so that children can record their observations.
5. When you are finished with the observations release the spider back outside.

WHAT IS A SPIDER?

WHAT THE CHILDREN WILL LEARN:
Spiders *(arachnids)* have 2 body parts and 8 legs.
Insects have 3 body parts and 6 legs.

YOU WILL NEED:
    One or two spiders in bug jars
    One or two insects in bug jars
    Magnifiers
    Paper, pencils, markers

TRY THIS!
1. Explain to the children that as they observe the spiders and insects they should look for how they are the same and how they are different.
2. The children can record their observations by writing or drawing on paper.
3. Record their observations on a graph.

	SPIDERS	INSECTS
# of legs		
# of body parts		
antennae (yes/no)		
other observations		

I'm a spider!

I'm an insect!

51

COLLECTING ABANDONED SPIDER WEBS

WHAT THE CHILDREN WILL LEARN:
Spider webs from the same species build the same web design. Spiders from different species build a different design.

YOU WILL NEED:
>Talcum Powder
>Spray adhesive (from a craft store)
>Black construction paper

TRY THIS!
1. Locate spider webs. Observe the web for a day to make certain it is an abandoned web.
2. Sprinkle talcum powder on the web.
3. Use the paper to lift the web carefully until the web is free and on the paper.
4. Spray with adhesive.
5. Collect different web designs if possible.
6. Caution the children to never touch a spider.

WHY DOES IT WORK?
Spiders' bodies secrete the sticky material needed to make a web. Each type of spider is born with the ability to make the web design particular to that type of spider.

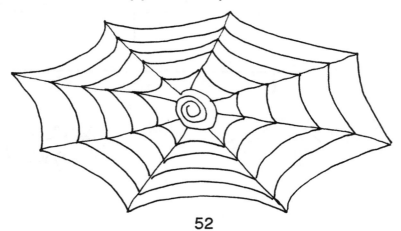

HOW SPIDERS FEEL VIBRATIONS

WHAT CHILDREN WILL LEARN:
Spiders can sense when an insect has been entrapped in the web. It can tell the size of the intruder by the intensity of the vibrations that the trapped insect sends along the web.

YOU WILL NEED:
    String
    A friend to help

TRY THIS!
1. Pull the string taut as you attach each end to a stationary object. (Like two chairs)
2. One partner places the tip of his/her finger gently on the end of one string.
3. While he/ she looks away, the other partner plucks the string at varying intensities--- lightly, medium and harshly.
4. See if the first partner can tell how hard the string has been plucked.
5. Switch places and try again.

WHY DOES IT WORK?
The vibrations travel down the full length of the string. A spider can tell by the intensity of vibrations on the web whether the trapped insect is too small, just right, or too large to eat.

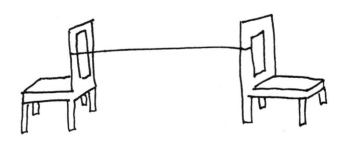

THEME INTEGRATION

Insects/Spiders
Animals
Food/Cooking

RELATED SONGS AND RHYMES

The Ants Go Marching
Arabella Miller
Eensy Weensy Spider
One Elephant

RELATED LITERATURE

The Very Busy Spider - Eric Carle
Be Nice to Spiders - Margaret Graham
Anansi the Spider - Gerald McDermott

MARY, MARY, QUITE CONTRARY

Mary, Mary, quite contrary,

How does your garden grow?

With silver bells and cockle-shells,

And pretty maids all in a row.

GROW A GARDEN

WHAT THE CHILDREN WILL LEARN:
Seeds need soil, water and sunlight in order to grow.

YOU WILL NEED:

 A bag of potting soil
 Cups or containers for planting
 Seeds (Try to find some silver bells,
  cockle-shells or pretty maids)
 Small shovels or spoons.
 Pencil (for poking a hole for the seed)
 Pitcher of water

TRY THIS!
1. Let each child scoop some potting soil into the container so that the soil is about 1 1/2 inches from the top.
2. Poke two or three holes in the soil 1 1/2 to 2 inches deep.(Check the seed package for the exact depth you'll need).
3. Place one seed in each hole.
4. Cover the hole with dirt.
5. Water lightly.
6. Place container near a sunny window. It often helps to cover it with plastic wrap until the seedlings come up.
7. Keep dirt moist by watering as frequently as needed.
8. Watch and compare which plants grow first, which grow tallest, which do not grow at all.

WHICH WAY IS UP?

WHAT THE CHILDREN WILL LEARN:
No matter how a seed is planted, the roots will go down
into the soil and the plant will reach up toward the sun.

WHAT YOU WILL NEED:
      Lima or Great Northern beans (Soak in water
           overnight)
      Paper towels
      Clear plastic cups
      Masking tape
      Permanent marker

TRY THIS!
1. Fold the paper towel in half.
2. Place the paper towel flat against the inside
    of the plastic cup.
3. Wad up another paper towel and place it inside the
    cup to hold the flat paper towel in place.
4. Wrap a piece of masking tape around the outside of
    the cup about 1" from the top.
5. Place 2-4 beans in the cup in between the cup and
    the paper towel.
6. Use the marker to indicate the direction each bean
    faces.
7. Keep the paper towel moist (not wet!) for seven days.
8. Observe in which direction the roots grow and the
    sprout grows.

WHY DOES IT WORK?
Roots grow toward the middle of the earth in search of
water and the stems grow upward in search of sunlight.
Regardless of the way the seeds are planted they will
follow this law of nature.

SWEATING LEAVES

WHAT THE CHILDREN WILL LEARN:
Plants lose water through their leaves in a process called *transpiration*.

YOU WILL NEED:
A healthy plant with leaves
Plastic bag
Tape

TRY THIS!
1. Place the plastic bag over one or several leaves.
2. Secure the bag around the leaf with tape.
3. Place the plant in a sunny window or in the sun for 2-3 hours.
4. Examine the water droplets inside the bag.

WHY DOES IT WORK?
Water is transported up the roots and through the tubes (*xylem*) in the stem. Up to 90% of that water is eventually lost through the pores (*stomata*) in the leaves in a process called *transpiration*. It is this water that is visible on the inside of the plastic bag.

TWO-COLORED FLOWER

WHAT THE CHILDREN WILL LEARN:
How water is transported through plant stems.

YOU WILL NEED:
> Measuring cup
> 2 glasses
> 1 white carnation with a long stem
> > (OPTION: one carnation per child)
> Blue and red food coloring
> 1 cup of water

blue   red

TRY THIS!
1. An adult cuts the stem of the carnation down the middle.
2. Fill each glass with 1/2 cup of water.
3. Add enough food coloring to get a deep color of red in one glass and a deep color of blue in the other.
4. Place one of the split stems in the red water and the other in the blue water.
5. Let the carnation stay in the water for 48 hours.
6. Observe the changes in the carnation.

WHY DOES IT WORK?
The carnation stem contains tubes called *xylem* which transports water up the stem and into the flower petals. Since this water contains color, that color is transported up the stem and into the flower petals. This is the same way that minerals in the soil are carried through the roots and into plant cells.

DISAPPEARING GREEN

<u>WHAT THE CHILDREN WILL LEARN:</u>
Without sunlight, grass cannot maintain the color green.

<u>YOU WILL NEED:</u>
   A patch of green grass
   A piece of cardboard or wood

<u>TRY THIS!</u>
1. Find a patch of grass outside or grow your own patch indoors in a pan.
2. Place a piece of cardboard or wood in one spot on the grass. Keep it there for 4-5 days.
3. After 4-5 days, lift up the cover and observe the changes in the grass. If it is not brown, continue to cover the grass for a few more days.
4. You can then remove the cover and observe how long it takes for the grass to grow back and regain the green color.

<u>WHY DOES IT WORK?</u>
Grass needs sunlight and oxygen to produce chlorophyll which provides the green color. Without oxygen and sunlight, the grass turns brown.

THEME INTEGRATION

Spring
Planting/Flowers
Colors
Day/Night
Water
Weather

RELATED SONGS AND RHYMES

The Green Grass Grew All Around
The Garden Song (Inch by Inch)
Oats and Beans and Barley Grow
Mulberry Bush

RELATED LITERATURE

The Tiny Seed - Eric Carle
The Legend of the Bluebonnet - Tomie de Paola
The Rose in My Garden - Arnold Lobel

ROSES ARE RED

Roses are red,
Violets are blue,
Sugar is sweet,
And so are you!

NOSE DETECTIVES

<u>WHAT THE CHILDREN WILL LEARN:</u>
Odors travel through the air and can be perceived by our sense of smell.

<u>YOU WILL NEED:</u>
> Something with a strong odor i.e. :
>> peeled onion
>> cotton ball soaked with perfume or vanilla or oil of wintergreen or clove
>> fresh coffee beans

<u>TRY THIS!</u>
1. In the classroom hide something with a strong odor.
2. Have the children search for the item using only their sense of smell.
3. After they have found it, discuss how they were able to discover the item without being able to see it.

<u>WHY DOES IT WORK?</u>
Odors travel through the air in the form of a gas. As children approach the hidden odor, the concentration of gas particles becomes heavier and the odor becomes stronger.

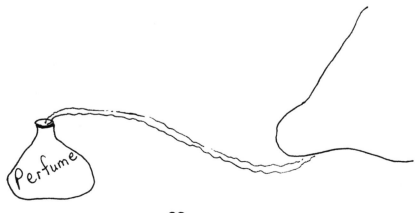

WHAT'S THAT SMELL?

<u>WHAT THE CHILDREN WILL LEARN:</u>
Children can identify many things by odor.

<u>YOU WILL NEED:</u>
Film canisters with holes punched in the top
Items with a strong smell i.e. :
rose petals, vanilla, coffee, lemon peel,
baby powder, cinnamon

<u>TRY THIS!</u>
1. Put tiny bits of the item with a smell in each canister (only one smell per canister!).
2. The children can sniff a canister and guess the smell.
3. Encourage them to find a friend with whom to compare answers.
4. If desired, you can write the answer or draw a picture of the item on a piece of paper glued to the bottom of the canister.

<u>WHY DOES IT WORK?</u>
The odors travel in the form of a gas. If it is an odor with which we are familiar, we can identify the smell without seeing the item. If we have never experienced the odor, we are unable to identify it by name but can still classify the smell as "good" or "bad".

WHAT'S MY TASTE?

WHAT THE CHILDREN WILL LEARN:
Some things that look the same taste completely different.

YOU WILL NEED:
    Salt and sugar
    Peeled potatoes and peeled apples
    Cocoa mix and unsweetened cocoa

TRY THIS!
1. Place the above items in separate bowls so that the children cannot tell their origin.
2. Show the children each of the sets of items they will taste and have them guess what each might be.
3. Let them taste each item one by one and watch the surprised looks on their faces.
4. Ask them to describe the tastes and textures.
5. *Variation:* Try other combinations of food that children can't identify by appearance i.e. lemon juice and lemonade.

WHY DOES IT WORK?
Through experience we learn to anticipate specific tastes that are typically associated with foods with which we are familiar. When the identifying factors such as food labels or fruit peels are removed, we often still anticipate what the taste may be. If it is something other than what is expected, the taste can be either a pleasant or unpleasant surprise!

COLOR MIXING

WHAT THE CHILDREN WILL LEARN:
When different colors are mixed together a new color is created.

YOU WILL NEED:
 Food coloring
 Clear plastic glasses or jars
 Droppers
 Water
 A pan for discarding water when finished

TRY THIS!
1. Fill several plastic containers or jars 2/3 full with water. Add several drops of food coloring to each glass to make each glass a nice deep color.
2. Give each child an empty clear plastic container and a dropper for individual color mixing.
3. Children can experiment making new colors by using the droppers to transfer colors from the original container to their own empty container.

WHY DOES IT WORK?
Since water and food coloring are soluble, the colors will mix together creating new colors:
 red + yellow= orange red + blue= purple
 blue + yellow= green red + green= brown

MAKE A RAINBOW

WHAT THE CHILDREN WILL LEARN:
Ink will separate into different colors.

YOU WILL NEED:
    Black and green water-soluble pens
    Coffee filters
    Small shallow dish or saucer
    Paper clip

TRY THIS!
1. Fold the coffee filter in half, then in half again, forming a cone.
2. Draw a short green line about one inch from the rounded end of the coffee filter.
3. Draw another line with the black marker near the green line but not touching.
4. Fill the dish or saucer with water.
5. Place the rounded edge of the cone in the water.
6. Let it stand for about one hour.
7. Observe how the colors have separated. You should see blue, yellow and purple from the black line and blue and yellow from the green line.

WHY DOES IT WORK?
All colors are made from three primary colors - red, blue, yellow. Black and green are combinations of colors. As the filter absorbs water, the ink begins to dissolve. The inks separate into the original colors that were combined to form black or green.

THEME INTEGRATION

Air/Wind
Colors
Five Senses (smell and taste)
Food/Cooking
Friends
Springtime / Flowers

RELATED SONGS AND RHYMES

"Colors" by Hap Palmer
"Everything Grows" by Raffi
The Garden Song

RELATED LITERATURE

The Tiny Seed - Eric Carle
The Rose in My Garden - Arnold Lobel
The Story of Ferdinand - Munro Leaf

THE NORTH WIND

The north wind doth blow,

And we shall have snow,

And what will poor Robin do then,

Poor thing?

He'll sit in a barn,

And keep himself warm,

And hide his head under his wing,

Poor thing.

MOVE THE BOOKS

WHAT THE CHILDREN WILL LEARN:
Air, when compressed, is strong enough to move heavy objects.

YOU WILL NEED:
    Balloon
    5-6 Books

TRY THIS!
1. Place a deflated balloon on a table with the neck of the balloon over the edge.
2. Put 5 or 6 medium size books on top of the balloon.
3. Blow up the balloon.
4. As the balloon inflates, the books lift and slide off to the side.

WHY DOES IT WORK?
When air is pushed into a contained space, the molecules stay close together, making the balloon strong. The air gives the books a powerful push forcing them to topple over.

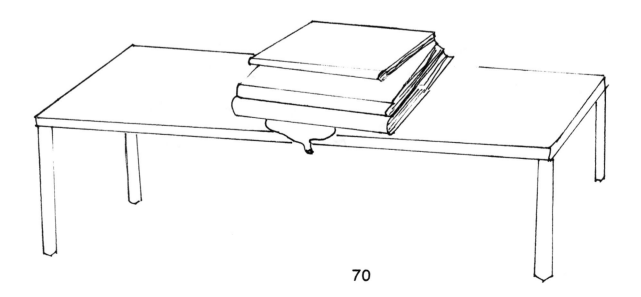

SINKING PAPER

WHAT THE CHILDREN WILL LEARN:
Less pressure under an object will create greater pressure above the object.

YOU WILL NEED:
  2 books (same size)
  Sheet of notebook paper
  Drinking straw

TRY THIS!
1. Place the books on a table about 4-5 inches apart.
2. Lay notebook paper across the books to make a bridge.
3. Hold the straw just under the edge of the paper.
4. Blow very hard.
5. The paper should sink in the middle toward the table.

WHY DOES IT WORK?
Air pressure around the notebook paper is equal when the air is still. The air pressure changes when air is blown under the paper . The rush of air reduces the pressure under the paper. Greater pressure is exerted onto the top of the paper forcing it to be pushed down toward the table.

CUPS AND STRAWS

WHAT THE CHILDREN WILL LEARN:
Air can be channeled into small spaces to move
specific objects.

YOU WILL NEED:
    Paper or Styrofoam cups (various sizes)
    Drinking straws
    Rope or string (optional)

TRY THIS!
1. Place a cup over the end of a straw.
2. Have the children try to get the cup off the
    straw without touching the cup.
3. Have children blow through the straw to force
    the cup straight up into the air.
4. Allow children time to experiment with the
    cup and straw. They could blow the cups
    back and forth to each other, catch the cups
    before they hit the ground, try to hit the
    ceiling with the cup, etc.
5. Attach the string to opposite sides of the room
    creating a fence. Try and blow the cups over
    the fence. Build a wall of cups. Blow the wall
    down.
6. Try using cups of different sizes. Will the effect
    be the same?

WHY DOES IT WORK?
Air is channeled into a narrow space. The force
of the air escaping from the straw causes the
objects near the air flow to move.

ROCKET LAUNCH

WHAT THE CHILDREN WILL LEARN:
Air forced from an object in one direction will move the object in the opposite direction.

YOU WILL NEED:
2 chairs   Balloon
String - 6-8 ft. long   Tape
Drinking straw   Air Pump
Picture of the Earth and the Moon (optional)

TRY THIS!
1. Push the string through the straw.
2. Tie the string to the two chairs. Separate the chairs until string is straight and tight.
3. Attach the picture of the Earth to one chair and the picture of the Moon to the other chair.
4. Tell the children that the straw is a rocket to be launched from the Earth to the Moon. The balloon will be the engine. Air will be the fuel.
5. Use the pump to blow up the balloon. Do not tie the end of balloon, but pinch it closed.
6. Keep the end pinched closed and hold the balloon under the straw. Tape the balloon to the straw with the opening pointing toward the picture of the Earth.
7. Countdown and launch the rocket by releasing the balloon. It should move along the string reaching the picture of the Moon.
8. Have children take turns launching the rocket either to the Moon or to Earth. Allow children to decide which way to turn the balloon to make the rocket launch.

WHY DOES IT WORK?
Air rushes out from the back of the balloon, forcing the balloon to be pushed forward. This shows opposite and equal reactions.

HELICOPTERS

WHAT THE CHILDREN WILL LEARN:
The shape of an object and the movement of air causes the object to spin.

YOU WILL NEED:
    Sheet of construction paper
    Paper clips

TRY THIS!
1. Trace the helicopter pattern onto construction paper. Cut on solid lines, fold on dotted lines.
2. Fold wings in opposite directions.
3. Fold handle up and attach a paper clip to the handle.
4. Holding the helicopter by the handle, throw it straight up into the air. It should spin as it falls to the ground.
5. Add additional paper clips to the handle of the helicopter. Will it spin faster, slower or simply crash?
6. Try bending the wings in the opposite direction. Does the helicopter spin to the right or the left?

WHY DOES IT WORK?
As the helicopter falls, air moves out from under the wings in all directions. The air hits the handle of the helicopter causing it to rotate.

fold in		
	fold in	
fold in		

THEME INTEGRATION

Air/Wind
Weather
Spring Time
Human Body
Simple Machines
Transportation

RELATED SONGS AND RHYMES

Rock-A-Bye Baby
The Wind
One Misty, Moisty Morning
Charlie's Bubble Box (from the record -
Machines and Things That Go by Jon Fromer)

RELATED LITERATURE

The Three Little Pigs - Paul Galdone
Hot Air Henry- Mary Calhoun
The Hat - Tomi Ungerer
The Wind Blew - Pat Hutchins

THREE MEN IN A TUB

Rub a dub dub,
Three men in a tub,
And how do you think
they got there?
The butcher, the baker,
The candlestick-maker,
They all jumped out of a
rotten potato.
'Twas enough to make a
man stare.

STRAWS AND POTATOES

WHAT THE CHILDREN WILL LEARN:
Closing the air inside a straw equalizes the pressure inside and out. This gives the straw extra strength as it is pushed into a potato.

YOU WILL NEED:
    Raw potato
    Drinking straws - about 4 inches long

TRY THIS!
1. Hold the straw and quickly try to push it into a potato. The straw should bend or collapse.
2. Try again, this time capping the top of the straw with your thumb.
3. Jab quickly at the potato. This time the straw should go in.

WHY DOES IT WORK?
When the top of the straw is left open, air rushes out of the straw, causing the straw to collapse. By closing the top of the straw, air is trapped inside, pushing against the sides of the straw. The air pressure outside is equal to the pressure inside the straw. The straw remains strong and plunges into the potato.

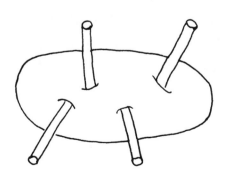

SALT WATER FISH

WHAT THE CHILDREN WILL LEARN:
Salt water weighs more than fresh water. An object floats in salt water because it weighs less than the salt water, but sinks in fresh water because it weighs more than the fresh water.

YOU WILL NEED:

    1/2 inch slice raw potato
    Colored cellophane -for fin and tail -(optional)
    2 liter bottle (cut the top off)
    Salt
    Blue food coloring

TRY THIS!
1. Fill 2 liter bottle with 3 cups water.
2. Add at least 10 large spoonfuls of salt. Stir to dissolve.
3. To 3 cups of non-salt water, add food coloring.
4. Slowly pour non-salt water into bottle of salt water. Salt water and fresh water should remain separate.
5. Add potato. It should sink through the fresh water but no deeper than the surface of the salt water.
6. Try other materials to see whether or not they float in fresh water, salt water or not at all.

WHY DOES IT WORK?
When salt is added to fresh water, the water level does not go up. Instead, the salt dissolves and the mixture fills the same space. The salt and the water join tightly together. Therefore, the density of the water increases. The weight (*density*) of the potato is less than the weight (*density*) of the salt water, but more than the fresh water.

FLOAT THE BOAT

WHAT THE CHILDREN WILL LEARN:
The shape of an object changes its weight. The more air an object has means less weight for the object. If it weighs less than the water, it will float.

YOU WILL NEED:
    Modeling clay
    Container of water

Which will sink?
Which will float?

TRY THIS!
1. Roll clay into a small ball.
2. Place the clay in water and watch it sink.
3. Flatten the clay out and place it on the surface of the water. The clay should float until water covers the top of the clay.
4. Curve the edges of the clay and seal it tightly to form a boat.
5. Place the boat in the water. The clay boat should float.

WHY DOES IT WORK?
Solid clay sinks because it weighs more than the water. Hollowing out the clay changes the weight (*density*) of the clay. The boat shape holds air which is less dense than the water so the boat floats. Both shape and weight (*density*) determine whether an object will sink or float.

SINK THE BOAT

WHAT THE CHILDREN WILL LEARN:
When weight is added to a boat, water moves up and around the boat. The boat will fill with water, become heavier than the water and sink.

YOU WILL NEED:
> Clay boat from previous experiment
> Boats made from a variety of materials -
>> aluminum foil, construction paper, plastic
> Container of water
> Various small objects - paper clips, toy people, washers, bolts, nuts, pieces of clay, etc. in sets of three

TRY THIS!
1. Place a boat into a container of water. Check to see how low the boat sits in the water.
2. Mark water level.
3. Slowly add three like objects into the boat. Has the water level changed?
4. Add three more objects. Note the change in water level.
5. Continue adding objects (by threes) until the boat begins to take on water and sink.
6. Do this with each type of boat to determine the order in which the boat sinks.
7. Keep a simple graph of how many objects were required to sink each type of boat.

WHY DOES IT WORK?
This is water displacement. As greater weight is added, the boat moves lower into the water. The water simply changes position, moving up and around the sides of the boat.

OCEAN IN A BOTTLE

<u>WHAT THE CHILDREN WILL LEARN:</u>
Certain substances do not mix together because they have different weights (*densities*).

<u>YOU WILL NEED:</u>

    Plastic 2-liter bottle
    Paint thinner
    Rubbing alcohol
    Food coloring

<u>TRY THIS!</u>
    These materials can be dangerous!
    Make the ocean without a child's help, and let
    them explore the finished product.
    <u>Always take extra care when working with rubbing
    alcohol and paint thinner.</u>

1. Fill a 2-liter bottle 1/3 of the way with rubbing alcohol.
2. Add food coloring and mix well.
3. Fill remaining 2/3 of bottle with paint thinner.
4. Replace cap and secure with tape so bottle may not be opened.
5. Turn bottle on to side and move bottle back and forth slowly.
6. Watch the waves form in the bottle. This is extremely soothing to watch!
7. If the "ocean" becomes too mixed up and cloudy, allow the bottle to sit for 30 minutes until contents have resettled.

<u>WHY DOES IT WORK?</u>
The alcohol and paint thinner will not mix. Alcohol molecules are tightly joined together, giving it a greater density than the paint thinner. The alcohol is heavy (*more dense*) and will settle to the bottom of the bottle while the paint thinner is lighter (*less dense*) and will separate from the alcohol.

THEME INTEGRATION

Food
Air/Wind
Community Workers
Containers
Transportation
Oceans
All About "3"

RELATED SONGS AND RHYMES

Three Little Kittens
I Saw A Ship A-Sailing
Three Blind Mice
Baa Baa Black Sheep
Rain, Rain Go Away
Pat-A-Cake
The Wise Men of Gotham
Aikendrum

RELATED LITERATURE

The Three Pigs - Lorinda Bryan Cauley
The Three Bears - Lorinda Bryan Cauley
Cloudy With A Chance of Meatballs -
Judi Barrett

TWINKLE, TWINKLE LITTLE STAR

Twinkle, twinkle, little star,

How I wonder what you are!

Up above the world so high,

Like a diamond in the sky.

Twinkle, twinkle, little star,

How I wonder what you are!

WHERE DO THE STARS GO?

<u>WHAT THE CHILDREN WILL LEARN:</u>
Stars are present, but not visible during the day because of the brightness of the sun.

<u>YOU WILL NEED:</u>
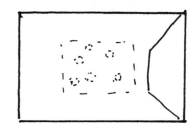
    White index card
    Hole punch
    White envelope
    Flashlight

<u>TRY THIS!</u>
1. Punch 8-10 holes in the index card.
2. Place card inside the envelope.
3. Shine the flashlight 2-3 inches in front of the envelope.
4. Next try shining the flashlight 2-3 inches behind the envelope. "Stars" should be visible.

<u>WHY DOES IT WORK?</u>
Light from the room, as well as the light from the flashlight, passes through the holes in the card when light comes in from the front. When the surrounding area is dark, the light passing through the holes is more easily seen. During the day, star light blends in with the light from the sun.

SHADOW DANCING

<u>WHAT THE CHILDREN WILL LEARN:</u>
Shadows are dark areas created by light hitting a solid object.

<u>YOU WILL NEED:</u>
> 8x10 ft. (or larger) white muslin sheet
> Overhead projector or film strip projector
> Variety of objects

<u>TRY THIS!</u>
1. Hang the muslin sheet from the ceiling. The sheet should touch the floor.
2. Turn on the projector so that the light hits the sheet from the back.
3. Hold various objects up to the light to create a shadow on the sheet.
4. Ask children to guess what object is being held.
5. Have several children stand, dance or just move around behind the sheet while the other children guess who they see.

The children will play behind the shadow screen for hours! Play dancing music and let the children have fun with shadows.

<u>WHY DOES IT WORK?</u>
Light cannot pass through a solid (*opaque*) object. When light hits an opaque object, it creates a dark area behind the object. This is a shadow.

MOVING SHADOWS

WHAT THE CHILDREN WILL LEARN:
The angle of light striking solid objects will create shadows of different lengths.

YOU WILL NEED:
    Chalk
    Concrete area
    A sunny day

TRY THIS!
1. Have the children work in pairs.
2. Go outside and have one child stand to create a shadow on the pavement.
3. Have the partner trace the shadow. (Switch places so both children get to have a shadow picture.)
4. Go back outside at different times during the day. Stand in the the same place and make another shadow picture.
5. Compare the shadows.

WHY DOES IT WORK?
As the Earth rotates during the day, light hits the Earth at different angles. During the early morning and late afternoon, the sun's rays hit the Earth at a low angle causing longer shadows. As the sun climbs to it highest point in the sky, light is cast almost straight down creating little, short shadows.

INVERTED LIGHT

<u>WHAT THE CHILDREN WILL LEARN:</u>
Light changes direction when it passes through a lens.

<u>YOU WILL NEED:</u>
    Flashlight or desk lamp
    Black construction paper
    Magnifying glass

<u>TRY THIS!</u>
1. Cut a simple picture (flower, tree, arrow) from the center of the black paper.
2. Attach the paper to the front of the flashlight or lamp.
3. Darken the room and shine the light 4-6 feet from a wall. The picture on the lamp should show up on the wall.
4. Hold the magnifying glass about 12 inches from the light source. Move the magnifying glass until a clear image forms on the wall.
5. The image should now be upside-down.

<u>WHY DOES IT WORK?</u>
Light travels in a straight line. When light hits the magnifying glass, the light changes directions. The image on the lamp goes from right-side-up to upside-down.

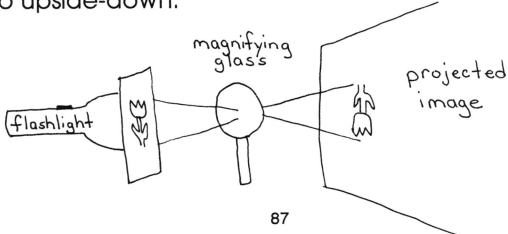

BOUNCING LIGHT

WHAT THE CHILDREN WILL LEARN:
Light bouncing off certain objects causes reflections.

YOU WILL NEED:
    Sunlight or flashlight
    Small hand mirrors

TRY THIS!
1. Hold the mirror so that it reflects the light from the sun or other light source onto a wall or floor.
2. Move the mirror slightly and watch the reflection move.
3. Children can experiment moving the reflection around the room. Try moving one reflection onto another reflection.
4. Play "Catch the Reflections".

WHY DOES IT WORK?
Light travels in a straight line. When light rays strike a smooth surface, the rays bounce off the surface at a matching angle. The light will then be reflected onto a different object.

THEME INTEGRATION

Day and Night
Light and Shadows
Outer Space/Gravity
The Sun
Time

RELATED SONGS AND RHYMES

Star Light, Star Bright
The Moon
"Journey Into Space" - Jane Murphy

RELATED LITERATURE

Moon Man - Tomi Ungerer
Sun Flight - Gerald McDermott
The Magic School Bus In Outer Space -
Joanna Cole

INDEX OF THEMES

AIR/WIND
I'm A Little Teapot
Humpty Dumpty
Jack and Jill
Jack Be Nimble
Roses Are Red
The North Wind
Three Men In A Tub

ANIMALS
Hey Diddle Diddle
Hickory Dickory Dock
Little Miss Muffet

COLORS
Humpty Dumpty
Mary, Mary, Quite Contrary
Roses Are Red

COMMUNITY WORKERS
Three Men In A Tub

CONTAINERS
Hickory Dickory Dock
I'm A Little Teapot
Jack and Jill
Three Men In A Tub

COUNTING
Three Men In A Tub

DAY/NIGHT
Mary, Mary, Quite Contrary
Twinkle, Twinkle Little Star

EGGS
Humpty Dumpty

FIVE SENSES
Hey Diddle Diddle
Roses Are Red

FLOWERS
Mary, Mary, Quite Contrary
Roses Are Red

FOOD/COOKING
Humpty Dumpty
I'm A Little Teapot
Little Miss Muffet
Three Men In A Tub
Roses Are Red

FRIENDS
Roses Are Red

HUMAN BODY
The North Wind

INSECTS/SPIDERS
Little Miss Muffet

LIGHT/SHADOWS
Jack Be Nimble
Twinkle, Twinkle Little Star

MATTER
I'm A Little Teapot

OCEANS
Three Men In A Tub

OUTER SPACE/GRAVITY
Humpty Dumpty
Jack and Jill
Twinkle, Twinkle Little Star

SIMPLE MACHINES
Hickory Dickory Dock
The North Wind

SPATIAL CONCEPTS
Hickory Dickory Dock

SPRING
Humpty Dumpty
Mary, Mary, Quite Contrary
Roses Are Red
The North Wind

TIME
Hickory Dickory Dock
Twinkle, Twinkle Little Star

TRANSPORTATION
Hickory Dickory Dock
The North Wind
Three Men In A Tub

WATER
Hey Diddle Diddle
I'm A Little Teapot
Jack and Jill
Mary, Mary, Quite Contrary

WEATHER
I'm A Little Teapot
Mary, Mary, Quite Contrary
The North Wind

SUGGESTED SCIENCE BOOKS

There are many good science books available through
the library and teacher supply stores.
Here are a few suggestions:

Bittinger, Gayle. **1-2-3 Science.** 1993.
Warren Publishing House, Inc.: Everett, WA.

Blackwelder, Sheila Kyser. **Science For All Seasons.**
1980. Prentice Hall: Englewood Cliffs, NJ.

McGavack, John. **Guppies, Bubbles & Vibrating
Objects.** 1969. John Day Co.: New York.

Van Cleave, Janice. **200 Gooey, Slippery, Slimy, Weird
& Fun Experiments.** 1993. John Wiley & Sons, Inc.:
New York.

Williams, Robert A. **Mudpies To Magnets.** 1987.
Gryphon House: Mt. Rainier, MD.

SUGGESTED BOOKS OF NURSERY RHYMES & POEMS

There are many good books of rhymes and poems
available through the library or book stores.
Here are a few of our favorites:

A Treasury of Mother Goose. 1984. Simon and Schuster:
New York.

Lobel, Arnold. **Whiskers And Rhymes.** 1985.
Greenwillow Books: New York.

Mark, Daniel; Editor. **A Child's Treasury of Poems.** 1986.
Dial Books for Young Readers: New York.

Prelutsky, Jack. **The Random House Book of Poetry for
Children.** 1983. Random House, Inc.: New York.

Notes

IF YOU BORROWED THIS BOOK... WHY NOT ORDER ONE FOR YOURSELF?

SCIENCE TIMES with NURSERY RHYMES.....................$16.95

OTHER GREAT PUBLICATIONS FROM

PANDA BEAR PUBLICATIONS

MUSIC EXPLOSION book and cassette...................................$39.95

Recipient of 1994 Early Childhood News Award
A complete early childhood curriculum, Music Explosion contains 34 classic childhood songs that introduce themes and activities across the curriculum. Includes an audio cassette and a large binder full of great activities for reading, math, science, art, literature, and more.

MUSIC MANIA book and cassette $29.95
MUSIC MANIA book and CD $34.95

Easy and fun ideas for teaching across the curriculum. Music Mania contains 26 favorite children's songs with over 500 activities in reading, math, science, art and literature. Make the musical connection to multiple intelligences!

THE CURIOSITY SHOP Idea Pack and cassette.....................$17.95
THE CURIOSITY SHOP Idea Pack and CD............................$21.95

Fantastic activities that encourage young children to think about and explore the world around them. Complete with the extremely popular *Curiosity Shop* CD or Cassette which is a wonderful collection of traditional and original songs chosen for their appeal to young children.

Title	Qty	Each	Total

SUBTOTAL	
CO res.add 3% sales tax	
Shipping & Handling add 15%	
TOTAL (must be in U.S. funds)	

Call Us or Mail or Fax this form to:
Panda Bear Publications;
 P.O. Box 391
Manitou Springs, CO 80829
Fax: (719) 685-4427
Phone: (719) 685-3319
www.pandabooks.com
e-mail: burtfam@ netscape.net

Name_____
Address_____
City, State, Zip_____
Phone (___) _____

I am paying with check, money order, MasterCard or Visa (circle one):
Credit Card #_____exp._____
Name on Card_____
Signature_____